T0193433

SURVIVING
THE
MONSTER

MARISOL PEREZ

authorHOUSE®

AuthorHouse™
1663 Liberty Drive
Bloomington, IN 47403
www.authorhouse.com
Phone: 1 (800) 839-8640

Published by AuthorHouse 07/25/2019

ISBN: 978-1-7283-1396-2 (sc)
ISBN: 978-1-7283-1395-5 (e)

PREFACE

Have you ever wondered why women stay in abusive relationships? Have you ever wondered why you yourself stay with your abuser? This book speaks about one young woman's story and how she escaped her abuser. She didn't make it out the first few times she tried to leave however, she did eventually. It takes a strong courageous person to leave an abusive partner. Jasmine walks you through her story and how she fought to make it out alive. There comes a time when as a woman we have to realize that we are stronger than we give ourselves credit for.

This book is for every woman who has ever been physically, emotionally, sexually, or verbally abused by their partner. This book isn't only for the victims though it is also, for their family members and friends who are trying to grasp what is truly going on. This book allows everyone to see how the victim feels and allows the victim to stop blaming themselves.

My goal in writing this book is to bring attention to the growing problem of domestic violence in this country. I also, want people to stop victim blaming the only person who is at fault is the abuser. The victim is just that the victim they don't deserve to be abused or threatened whether physical or verbal. Jasmine brings the reality of the situation to light and I hope other women in similar circumstances can find hope in Jasmine's story.

In the world today we seem to be taking away women's rights, domestic violence laws are being stripped down to nothing and are becoming more lenient yet the number and severity of domestic violence attacks are increasing. If this book can help even one woman than it was worth all of the long hours and sleepless nights that I have poured into this book. I hope I never have to hear about another Jasmine on the news. It breaks my heart every time I hear about a husband getting angry and killing his wife and kids. I have flash backs every time I think about the woman whose fiancé killed her because she no longer wanted to be with him. Every time I hear these stories of women trying to leave and being killed it makes me realize how much worse Jasmine's story could have been.

When a woman decides to leave her abuser and actually takes the steps to follow through with that plan it can be one of the most dangerous times for her. It is important to have a plan in place and to have a support system set up. If you don't have a support system, it is important to know where you are going and to make sure that no one else knows where you are headed. You in a sense have to keep your plan a secret. My hope is for all women to learn from Jasmine's mistakes and to not end up in her shoes.

Domestic Violence is a cycle it never ends. There may be happy times, but there will also be times that are a complete nightmare. During the cycle you have the build up phase where tension builds and continues to grow until the person has complete control and fear from their victim. Then you have the explosion phase where the abuser abuses and beats the victim. Then you have the remorse phase where they apologize and justify their actions. Then you have the phase where they make promises and plans for your future and lastly the honeymoon phase where things seems completely perfect before the cycle starts again. In domestic violence situations there is always a phase where the abuser apologizes and then the honeymoon phase where everything is fine for a while. During this time he may buy you flowers, nice gifts and make you feel special. Ladies please don't allow yourselves to fall victim to this never-ending cycle.

Whenever I think of domestic violence, I always think about that Facebook post where the woman received flowers not because he beat her that day, not because it was her birthday or Mother's Day, but because her abuser finally killed her. I can't imagine the pain my family would have went through if I had allowed myself to be a statistic. I can't imagine the pain other families feel when their loved ones are killed by a senseless act of violence. Let's end this vicious cycle of violence and take a stand to end the cycle of domestic violence. Don't be afraid to speak up, ask for help and get out!

CHAPTER ONE

LOVE AT FIRST SIGHT

At seventeen the typical teenage girl thinks she knows everything. Jasmine was no different; she was graduating in a little over a month and had been accepted to a handful of colleges. Jasmine was an amazing student she always brought home A's and B's. Her senior year her grades weren't as great because she struggled with Precalculus and Physics GT. However, she kept her GPA up with her other courses she managed to pull A's in those.

Jasmine was the oldest of six children in a blended family. In high school Jasmine played the flute, was in the school color guard, and ran a mentoring program that partnered high school students at her school with students at two local elementary schools. During her senior year Jasmine mentored students five days a week after school and worked part time at the library. Jasmine wasn't your typical high school teenager. She didn't feel as though she fit in at school, she hated the cliques and stereotypes. She tried to be friends with everyone and anyone she didn't care that she wasn't popular or smart enough to be considered a nerd. She honestly had no real friends because she disliked the childishness of those around her.

Jasmine had always been wise beyond her years. She grew up in a broken home and knew what could happen when love went wrong. She just wanted to focus on her studies. Everyday Jasmine got up and went to school. After school she came home put her stuff down, grabbed a snack and headed out the door to go to mentor local students. After mentoring she would wait for her little brother to get out of school and walk him home. Once home Jasmine would get ready for work and do homework if she had time.

One day while Jasmine was walking to mentor students at the local elementary school, she heard someone trying to get her attention. "Hey shorty!" they called. Jasmine hated that. She absolutely hated when guys tried to get her attention through catcalling. Once the young man realized Jasmine wasn't going to acknowledge him, he approached her and spoke. "Hi, how are you today?" he said. The two chatted for a moment, then exchanged names and numbers. Jasmine learned from their chat that his name was Thomas and that he had recently moved to the area from New York. Jasmine then went on to mentor her students before heading to work.

Later that evening Thomas and Jasmine began texting each other. Jasmine really liked Thomas he seemed sweet and caring from his text messages. Thomas began walking Jasmine to mentoring and meeting up with her after she finished since she still had to wait for her little brother to get out of class. On the days her students were absent from school Jasmine began hanging out with Thomas at his house. On one occasion the two began making out and it was at this point Thomas asked Jasmine if she wanted to have sex then or wait a while longer. Jasmine said she wanted to wait until after she graduated high school and Thomas agreed. Thomas's family adored Jasmine. His family believed Jasmine was eighteen because Thomas was twenty-five turning twenty-six in June, so Thomas told his family that jasmine was already eighteen.

Jasmine enjoyed hers and Thomas's time together. Before long she was getting ready to graduate from high school. During the summer before high school Jasmine spent time with her friend Candace and Thomas. Because Candace and Jasmine worked conflicting work schedules sometimes Jasmine would sometimes hangout with Thomas until Candace got off from work. Thomas and Jasmine would spend time talking, watching movies, and joking around. Eventually they decided to have sex. Jasmine was head over heels for Thomas. She was truly in love with him, or so she thought.

A few weeks later Jasmine had to have surgery. She wouldn't see Thomas or be able to talk to him for four weeks. She couldn't work for two weeks either. She had surgery to remove all four of her wisdom teeth and her lower jaw was surgically broken due to TMJ. Jasmine couldn't eat real food for weeks. She missed talking to Thomas and he missed her as well. Once Jasmine was healed, she was ready to get back to work and spending time with Thomas. Jasmine was starting college in just a couple of weeks at the University of Alexandria.

Jasmine and Thomas enjoyed all their time together. Eventually August came and Jasmine started school. Jasmine was enrolled in school full time, working at the local library part time, and working one evening a week at the library on campus. Jasmine and Thomas began spending time together on the weekends. Jasmine's parents once again thought she was with Candace. Jasmine wasn't spending enough time with Thomas in her mind. She began skipping school to spend time with Thomas.

Eventually Jasmine's mom caught her skipping school. Jasmine was supposed to call or text her mom when she made it to school. Jasmine forgot to text her mom around 8:45 that morning to let her know she made it. When her mom couldn't reach her, she called the school and spoke to Jasmine's professor. She learned Jasmine never showed up for class. When Jasmine did call her mom, she was livid. She demanded to know where Jasmine was. Jasmine quickly walked over to a female friend's house so her mom could pick her up there. Jasmine was in trouble she was grounded. At this point Jasmine was eighteen.

In Jasmine's mind she was an adult and her mom couldn't dictate what she was doing. Jasmine was annoyed she began thinking of ways to see Thomas. Jasmine began telling her parents she had to work then going to Thomas's house to hang out and getting back to the library in time for her dad to pick her up from "work". One night though Jasmine's dad sent her grandmother to pick her up. Jasmine didn't get back there early enough because her grandmother was always thirty minutes early. Her grandmother caught her, and Jasmine lied to her, she told her she had been working the whole night. Her grandmother let it go, but she knew in heart Jasmine was lying.

Jasmine was relieved until her grandmother said something to her mom. Then as if that wasn't bad enough a local police officer told Jasmine's dad who she was dating. Her dad was furious. Now Jasmine's dad never wanted his daughter to end up with a black man. The fact that Thomas was black was partially why Jasmine didn't want her parents to know she was dating. At this point Jasmine was given a choice to live by her parent's rules or to find somewhere else to live. Jasmine knew she would be permanently grounded at this rate.

CHAPTER TWO

MOVING OUT

Jasmine was with Candace when her parents called with their ultimatum. Candace was in shock. Candace called her mom and dad and asked if Jasmine could stay there, they agreed. Candace and Jasmine went to Jasmine's dad's house and got her things. Jasmine's dad was upset that she was choosing Thomas.

Jasmine didn't care; she moved in with Candace and her family. She continued going to school and working at the local library. Now since she wasn't living with her parent's she didn't have to sneak around to see Thomas. Jasmine attended school every day. Jasmine spent time with Thomas on the weekends. Things were great between Thomas and Jasmine, his family adored her.

One afternoon while Candace was working Jasmine stayed with Thomas. The plan was once Candace got off, they were going to grab dinner and go to sleep, they both had class the next morning. However, while Thomas and Jasmine were hanging out something happened.

Thomas's cousin Brittany was visiting from New York. She felt that she should be allowed in Thomas's room whenever she wanted. Brittany is the type of female that looks, dresses, and acts like a man. Brittany had an attitude because Thomas didn't want her in his room. He had Jasmine over, they wanted alone time, they wanted to have sex. Thomas and Jasmine were horsing around on the bed. The room was very small, and Brittany was sitting on a chair maybe a foot from the bed. Jasmine's foot brushed against Brittany's arm.

Brittany snapped. She jumped up and grabbed Jasmine. Thomas's first instinct was to protect Jasmine so Brittany wouldn't seriously injure her. Thomas accidentally busted Brittany's lip in the scuffle. Thomas took Jasmine outside and they decided it would be best if Jasmine left for the evening. Jasmine called her friend Vicki and walked to her house until Candace got off.

When Jasmine got to Vicki's house they hung out in her room and talked to Vicki's boyfriend on the phone. Then Jasmine's leg started to hurt, so she looked at it. Jasmine had a huge bruise and due to how quickly the situation spiraled Jasmine had no clue how it happened. She wasn't sure if Brittany hit her or if it was from hitting the hardwood floor. Her thigh was black and blue and Jasmine knew it would take weeks to heal.

Thomas called later that night to apologize for what had happened. Jasmine knew it wasn't his fault. At this point he was Jasmine's knight in shining armor. He protected her from his cousin. He stood up to his own flesh and blood to protect Jasmine. Jasmine was impressed.

Candace eventually got tired of Jasmine living with her. Her family began to compare her to Jasmine, and she felt her family liked Jasmine more. This time Jasmine had no idea where she would go. She couldn't afford her own place. Jasmine stayed with Thomas for about a week. Then they spoke to her friend Frank's dad, John, about her moving in with him.

John agreed to let Jasmine move in. He gave Jasmine his room as his room was the only room with a bathroom inside and the only room with a door. John never slept in his room anyway, he was an alcoholic and constantly passed out on the couch. What Jasmine didn't realize before moving in was that this house was a trap house (a house drugs are stored and sold). Jasmine moved in and took over the master bedroom. She never spent the night there alone, Thomas was always with her.

Jasmine was able to come and go as she pleased from the house. John enjoyed having her there it was almost as though it reminded him of having his own daughter living at home again. Jasmine and John had a great relationship. They would joke around about how ignorant some of the guys were that would come and go from the house. John wanted Jasmine to feel safe in the house and he did everything he could to make sure she knew she was safe.

CHAPTER THREE

THE MONSTER MAKES AN APPEARANCE

Jasmine woke up one morning and John had left work. Jasmine was home with Thomas and his friends. Jasmine got up and got dressed and went down to the living room and sat on the couch. Jasmine threw on a pink tank top and jean shorts because it was 80 degrees outside. Thomas noticed one of his friends was staring at Jasmine. He demanded that she change her clothes. Jasmine refused and told Thomas he was acting silly. Thomas gave Jasmine the nastiest look before walking across the room and slapping her across the face so hard she fell to the ground. Jasmine went upstairs, closed her door, and cried her eyes out. She sat in her room and tried to piece together what had happened. Jasmine thought to herself maybe I should have changed my clothes. Why didn't I just listen to him? Why didn't I just change my clothes? These were the thoughts running through her head. Jasmine never told anyone that Thomas slapped her because she was worried, they wouldn't believe her.

After everyone left Thomas came upstairs and apologized. He told Jasmine that Daniel had been staring at her and he didn't like it. Thomas told Jasmine he was afraid she would leave him for someone smarter than him. Jasmine was beginning to realize that Thomas was insecure, so she tried reassuring Thomas the best she could that she wasn't going anywhere.

A few weeks later Thomas had his friend Benny over the house. Benny and Thomas were talking business, but Jasmine was hungry and needed to eat. She went to Thomas and told him she was hungry. He asked her to give him five minutes. He said Benny would drive them McDonalds to get something to eat. Jasmine waited for twenty minutes no one had gone anywhere. Benny lit a marijuana joint. Jasmine asked him if was driving Thomas and her to McDonalds. Benny told Jasmine he wasn't driving her anywhere she could walk, however, he would give Thomas a ride. Jasmine was furious.

Jasmine went to Thomas and asked him to give her some money. Thomas handed Jasmine some money and continued his phone conversation. Jasmine stormed upstairs slamming the basement door behind her. John heard the door slam and got up to see what was going on. He could see that Jasmine was upset so he gave he a hug and asked her what happened. When Jasmine told John, what had unfolded in the basement he was mad. After all it was his house and Jasmine was the only woman that stayed there so he expected everyone to respect her. John told his son, Frank, to walk with Jasmine to get food.

John refused to let Jasmine leave without Frank going with her. On the way to McDonald's Frank and Jasmine talked about what had unfolded at the house. Frank apologized because he knew that what Benny did was wrong. As they passed Thomas's house his cousin Stephanie began asking Jasmine questions. Jasmine explained to Stephanie that Benny was rude to her. Stephanie was shocked. Stephanie couldn't believe that Benny had spoken to Jasmine in such a disrespectful way Jasmine told her that she had left Thomas and Benny at Frank's house together.

Jasmine and Frank finally made it to McDonalds and got something to eat. They then walked back towards the house. On the way back Thomas called Jasmine to see where she was. Frank and Jasmine met up with Thomas. Frank warned Thomas to keep his hands to himself. Jasmine and Thomas talked about what had happened at John's house. Jasmine and Thomas continued walking back towards Thomas's house while talking about what happened. Thomas didn't understand why Jasmine stormed out, but once she explained what Benny said Thomas understood. Jasmine and Thomas were both fine and not mad at one another.

Once they rounded the corner by Thomas's house Benny started yelling and aggressively approaching Jasmine. Thomas walked away. Jasmine felt as though she had been set up to be attacked by Benny. Frank immediately jumped in he wasn't going to stand by and watch this man again verbally abuse Jasmine. Frank was only sixteen years old and when he spoke up Benny began threatening him.

When Kevin heard Benny yelling and screaming, he put his cigarette out and walked back across the street to see what was going on. When Kevin heard Benny threatening Frank and Jasmine, he pulled him aside and told him he needed to leave.

Kevin then went to speak to Thomas. Kevin told Thomas that whenever Benny is around, he changes who he is. Kevin asked Thomas, "Since when do you let someone speak to Jasmine like that? Why is a sixteen-year-old kid defending your girlfriend when you are right here?" Kevin told him he really needed to get his priorities in order. He also, told Thomas that he needed to stop letting your so called friends define how you behave.

While Kevin and Thomas talked Jasmine left with Frank and went home. Once they got back to the house Jasmine went up to her room to sit and think. She wanted to be left alone. Jasmine was a sweet girl and couldn't believe the way she was being treated. She almost felt like a prisoner in her own life.

Later that evening Thomas came over to see Jasmine. Thomas once again apologized for his behavior. Jasmine was still upset, but she forgave Thomas and pretended everything was okay.

CHAPTER FOUR

ALCOHOL OVERLOAD

A few days later Thomas bought a bottle of Hennessy. His cousins came over and played cards with him in Jasmine's room while they drank liquor. Thomas poured Jasmine a shot she drank the shot with coke as a chaser. Jasmine woke up fine the next morning and went to work.

The following day Thomas purchased a bottle of tequila. When he got back to the house, he took a shot with Jasmine and poured some more into a cup for her. He had to go out to make a drug deal and he promised to be back soon. By the time Thomas returned Jasmine had drank a quarter of the bottle. Kevin told Thomas not to give Jasmine anything else to drink. Everyone was starting to worry she may get alcohol poisoning. Jasmine was only 100 pounds at the time, Thomas took Jasmine upstairs and poured her another drink. That is the last thing Jasmine remembers.

The next morning when Jasmine woke up, she found herself on the floor of her bedroom, she was naked and cold. Jasmine couldn't figure out how she had gotten there. She knew she had a lot to drink the night before, but Jasmine had completely blacked out and couldn't remember anything.

A few years later Jasmine was told that she fell down the stairs that night. Someone else told her that yes, she did fall down the stairs and that she had also had sex with at least four men that night. Jasmine was crushed how did she not know this had happened. That's when Jasmine remembered that she had heard stories of Thomas and friends slipping drugs into girl's drinks.

Jasmine recalled one night that Kelly, a girl from Jasmine's high school came over. Kelly seemed completely unaware of what was going on around her to the point she started putting Jasmine in danger. Jasmine had been in bed before Kelly arrived with no clothes on. Kelly burst into the room and took her shoes off and dropped her purse on the floor next to them. She then went downstairs with the guys. Jasmine remained upstairs in her room. About an hour later Kelly came back upstairs to gather her things. When she came back upstairs, she left Jasmine's door wide open. Jasmine felt very vulnerable she was naked and there was a group of four men outside her bedroom door all peeking in.

Once Kelly left the room Jasmine asked Thomas if Kelly was drunk. That's when Thomas told Jasmine that the guys had put ecstasy in Kelly's drink so they could have their way with her. Jasmine was disappointed. She told Thomas that what they did was wrong and dangerous. Jasmine felt bad about being annoyed with Kelly for putting her danger.

Jasmine never thought in a million years this same thing could or would happen to her with Thomas around.

Once Jasmine got up, she began getting ready for work. At this point Jasmine was working two jobs and she had quit going to school. Jasmine was working at both the local library and at Victoria's Secret. The women Jasmine worked with thought Thomas was a catch. He would bring Jasmine to work he would find her rides home. Little did her coworkers know that this was his way of controlling Jasmine's every move.

After she started drinking Jasmine's periods were horrible. Her stomach would become distended and she would have horrible cramps. Jasmine would spend a lot of her time curled up in the fetal position. Jasmine began to self-medicate with Motrin. Before long Jasmine couldn't take the pain anymore and called her pediatrician. They recommended alternating the Motrin 800's with Aleve. When she went in for an appointment, they ordered an ultrasound to figure out why she was in so much pain. They called her a few days later to tell Jasmine she had a few cysts and they should clear up on their own.

SECOND

CHAPTER FIVE

TIME TO MOVE

Jasmine came home from work one night to find out that John's house was being foreclosed on. She had exactly one month to find somewhere else to live. Kevin, Jasmine, and Thomas came up with a plan. The three of them would rent an apartment together. Kevin and Jasmine started figuring out what they could afford as the apartment would need to be in their names. Kevin wanted to stay in the same area on the same side of town. Jasmine didn't really care she knew the next county over was a little bit cheaper for rent.

About one week after John was evicted from the house Jasmine and Kevin were approved for an apartment. They were even able to move in a few days early. The day that they moved Thomas, Kevin, and Jasmine were walking from the apartment to Thomas's aunt's house. Thomas had to meet a customer along the way. The local police in the area were having a community fair and there were officers everywhere.

Thomas dropped the marijuana into a hole in the ground as Kevin and Jasmine stood watch. The plan was for Jasmine and Kevin to go to Thomas's aunt's house while he walked with his customers to the liquor store to get some beer. As Kevin and Jasmine were walking away, they looked up to see a man pulling a beaded chain from underneath his shirt. "Stop" he yelled. Jasmine and Kevin froze in their tracks. That's when the officer released them. He wanted Thomas.

Him and his partner had seen the kids give Thomas money. Jasmine stood around a corner in dismay watching the police practically strip Thomas in broad daylight. They pulled Thomas's jeans down to get to his shorts. They then forced him to take his shoes off and then they sat him down and handcuffed him. Jasmine was worried that Thomas was going to be arrested. Jasmine was terrified that the officer would find the drugs. That's when Kevin reminded her that there is no way they would find them because who would think to look in a hole in the ground.

Eventually the officers finished with Thomas and he went back to his aunt's house to get Jasmine. The two of them then started walking back to their apartment. When once again they were stopped by the same two police officers. The officers wanted to speak with Jasmine this time. They said they needed to verify her age because according to them Jasmine looked like she was twelve. The officers told Thomas to leave or they would arrest him for providing them with a false name in their previous encounter. Thomas left and had his cousin Stephanie return with Jasmine's identification. The officers reviewed Jasmine identification and told her that Thomas was a bad influence and then released her.

Jasmine didn't heed the officers warning. A few days later Jasmine went and spent the night at her mom's in Alexandria, so she could grab a few things from her old room for the apartment. While she was gone Thomas and Kevin had a party at the apartment. The next morning when Jasmine got back into Alexandria, she called Thomas to help her take everything over to the apartment. Thomas met Jasmine at her dad's house and together they carried Jasmine's stuff to the apartment.

Once everything was settled in the apartment Jasmine and Thomas laid back down to sleep. Around 10:00 AM Brittany woke Jasmine and Thomas to tell them there were two men at the door asking to speak to Jasmine. Jasmine quickly put on clothes and went to the door. The two men were narcotics detectives and had obtained a warrant to search the apartment. Jasmine didn't think anything of it she had already told Thomas and Kevin not to keep any drugs in the apartment. After conducting a search of the apartment, the two detectives spoke to Jasmine telling her they found two dime size bags of marijuana as well as paraphernalia. Jasmine was furious she was in school to be a teacher and this was going to ruin it.

Thomas immediately admitted to the office that the drugs and paraphernalia was his and the detectives told Jasmine they knew it was because they found it in his closet. The detectives then placed Thomas under arrest. At the same time, they told Brittany she needed to leave the residence. Brittany tried to resist as she wanted to stay with Jasmine in her mind there was no need to arrest Jasmine because Thomas had already claimed possession. Once Brittany was out the door the detectives called for a female officer.

Once the female officer arrived on scene the detectives told her they were placing Jasmine under arrest. The officer gave the detectives a confused looked since she heard Thomas claimed possession. She knew that Jasmine's charges would be dismissed by a judge more likely than not at court. However, the officer stayed quiet she patted Jasmine down and placed her in cuffs. The detectives then asked her to take Thomas down to central booking because they weren't done with Jasmine.

Once alone with the two detectives they informed Jasmine of her rights. They told Jasmine they would let her go if she bought marijuana from someone and let them watch her do it. Jasmine didn't smoke though, and she knew that if she went and asked anyone for marijuana it was going to get her into a different kind of trouble. Not to mention Jasmine had no clue where to get it. Jasmine told the detectives that she didn't do drugs. The detectives didn't believe her they didn't want to hear anything she said they continued trying to get Jasmine to flip on anyone. Jasmine never broke instead she told the detectives," You want me to buy drugs from someone fine I will. You tell me who to buy them from and I will do it." The detectives looked at Jasmine confused they told her well you must know the person if you have never done this before it won't work. The detectives looked defeated they then took Jasmine down to central booking.

Once down at central booking Thomas and Jasmine were seated next to each other. Thomas kept telling Jasmine how sorry he was. Jasmine was so livid all she could do was tell him to shut up, she cursed at him, and told him to leave her alone. She repeated herself for what felt like a million times. The arresting detectives eventually told Thomas to shut up. Thomas didn't know how to shut up though, so he continued apologizing. Thomas kept talking so much they told him that they were going to hold on to his file for a few hours before giving it to the commissioner. This made Jasmine uneasy because she needed a ride home and she was going to call Thomas's aunt for a ride.

Jasmine was nervous and mad at the same time. She tried to keep calm. All she could think about is who Thomas and Kevin had in the house the night before. Who would have said something to the police? Only one name came to mind. Jasmine finally went to see the commissioner who released her on her own recognizance. Once released Jasmine collected her phone and belongings and began waiting for Thomas.

About forty-five minutes later Thomas was released on his own recognizance. After they were both released, they went to find a payphone because Jasmine's cell phone was dead. Thomas's aunt wasn't happy about the situation and she of course found a way to blame Jasmine. Jasmine was just lucky that it was her day off from work she didn't want a no call no show on her record.

Jasmine and Thomas almost immediately began talking to lawyers. Since Jasmine was in school to become a teacher, she couldn't have any charges on her record. Jasmine and Thomas spoke to one lawyer who told her the best option was the stet dot program where she would have to take classes and submit to random drug screenings for a period of three months and then after that she would stay out of trouble for one year and her record would be eligible to be expunged.

A few days later Kevin and Jasmine received an eviction notice which they already knew was coming. Jasmine didn't know where she would go next, she was already working two jobs and in school and could barely make enough money to make ends meet.

During the rest of the month in the apartment things between Thomas and Jasmine took a turn for the worst. Jasmine didn't know what to do or how to feel. Jasmine made another appointment at the doctor to get the results of her ultrasound. When she went for her appointment, they asked her if she smoked. She told them no. They gave her a breathing treatment because she was wheezing from all the secondhand smoke in the apartment. They then referred her to and OB/GYN because she had cysts on both of her ovaries and that was what was causing her distended abdomen and pain.

When Jasmine got back to the apartment, she told Thomas that no one could smoke in the apartment. Jasmine ended up borrowing her little sisters' nebulizer so she could do a few more breathing treatments at the apartment alone. Thomas hated the sound of the machine. He later told Jasmine that it reminded him of the machines his grandmother was connected to before she passed away. Jasmine understood that it brought back bad memories and hoped that it would ensure that no one smoke in the apartment.

A few days later Thomas got a call that his brother had been arrested in a federal investigation in New York. When this happened Thomas's, world came crashing down. That night Jasmine spent much of her time trying to console him. She told him things would be okay and she tried to make him feel at ease. Despite her trying Thomas was wound tight. He sat at the foot of the bed in a chair just staring. Jasmine tried to convince Thomas to just come to bed and get some sleep. Instead what Jasmine got was a slap across the face. Jasmine laid there and cried herself to sleep. Did Thomas just slap her because his feelings are hurt and Jasmine cares enough to try to help him?

The next morning as Jasmine got ready for work and school Thomas apologized. Jasmine accepted his apology what else could she do. Jasmine left for school for a few hours then worked a closing shift at Victoria's Secret. When Jasmine got home, Thomas told her that he and Kevin were going out of town with his family for a week for their family reunion in South Carolina.

Jasmine was nervous she told Thomas that she didn't want to stay at the apartment alone she didn't feel safe. Thomas recommended that she have James and Oscar stay with her as they needed somewhere to crash anyway. The first day that Thomas was gone James made sure Jasmine got home from work safely. He met her at the apartment after her shift to let her in since he had her house keys. The next night they did the same thing. When Jasmine got home from work the second night Oscar had a friend over. Jasmine came in and showered and put on shorts and a t-shirt. She knew James and Oscar weren't looking at her they had become like brothers to her.

Jasmine went to put a load of laundry in the washer. When she walked past Oscar's friend, Tony, he grabbed her arm. Oscar saw it and glared at Tony. "That's Thomas's girl" Oscar said. Tony apologized. Jasmine told James she wasn't feeling well and that she was going to lay down. Jasmine was in pain from the cysts on her ovaries.

A few hours later Thomas called to check on Jasmine and to speak with James. James nor Jasmine knew Tony was still in the house as they had both been woken up by Thomas's call. After hanging up with Thomas Jasmine worked on some homework. A few minutes after starting her homework Oscar knocked on the door. Jasmine told him to come in. Oscar asked to borrow Jasmine's charger and she agreed.

Jasmine finished her homework within an hour and laid back down. Shortly after laying back down Oscar came back into Jasmine's room to return the borrowed charger. He plugged Jasmine's phone in and closed her door tight on his way out. The next morning Jasmine awoke to Tony knocking on her bedroom door. Tony told Jasmine that she had left her credit cards in the bathroom and she shouldn't leave them laying around. Jasmine responded by telling Tony that both James and Oscar would never steal from her, so she wasn't worried about her cards being in the bathroom.

Jasmine went back to sleep she awoke for a second time to the feeling of someone watching her. Tony was sitting in her room by the window drinking a glass of orange juice. He offered Jasmine a glass. Jasmine told him no and told him he needed to get out of her room. Forty-five minutes later Jasmine woke up to Tony trying to climb in bed with her. Jasmine quickly jumped up and ran out of her room to wake James.

Jasmine found James asleep on the floor in the living room and began kicking him awake. James jumped up and ran outside behind Tony. James sent Jasmine to wake up

Oscar to tell him what happened. Oscar was just as mad. James got up and walked Jasmine to get breakfast from McDonalds across the street. After that they went back home, and Jasmine got ready for work. James's cousin, Sean offered to drive Jasmine to work and he spoke with James and Jasmine about the incident and told them they needed to come clean to Thomas.

Later that evening when Jasmine got home from work, she needed to walk to the store to buy groceries. She cut thru her apartment complex and walked to the local Kroger's. On her way back from the store Jasmine decided to take the short cut behind the liquor store. Tony and his friends were standing there on the path. Tony was mad that everyone knew what he had done to Jasmine so he tried to pick a fight with her thinking she would apologize to him. Instead Jasmine did the opposite. Jasmine embarrassed him again in front of his friends. She put her groceries down and stood their fists clenched. She asked Tony why he tried to get in bed with her. He quickly said that he didn't try to get in bed with Jasmine. Jasmine asked, "Well what were you doing then? When I woke up you were next to me in my bed partially under my blankets? But you say you weren't in my bed I am confused." Tony's face went blank. He didn't know what to say. Jasmine wasn't backing down and two of Thomas's friends were there and they stepped between Tony and Jasmine. Jasmine left and went home while the guys began to question Tony about his actions.

Later that evening James and Jasmine decided that they needed to tell Thomas what had happened. They called Thomas together. Thomas began calling Jasmine a slut bucket and a whore. Jasmine was devastated. Thomas was calling her mean and hurtful names when she had done nothing wrong. James felt guilty to the point her refused to stay at the apartment with Jasmine anymore. So, she spent the night alone by herself. Jasmine was miserable she didn't want to be alone. The next day after work Jasmine was walking home and ran into Frank. Jasmine was ecstatic. Frank was looking for his dad, who was still homeless from the eviction. To make matters worse some of the local teenagers had jumped Franks dad and he had been in the hospital, but recently discharged.

Since Frank had nowhere to crash Jasmine offered up her apartment. Jasmine explained to Frank what had happened the night before. Frank was livid that everyone abandoned Jasmine. Frank stayed the night with Jasmine and even slept in her room with her so that she wasn't alone. Jasmine was afraid Tony would come back. Frank promised Jasmine that nothing would happen to her while he was there. Frank and his dad ended up staying with Jasmine until Thomas and Kevin got back from South Carolina.

Once Thomas and Kevin got back Thomas turned even more abusive. They only had a few more weeks left in the apartment. Once Thomas and Kevin arrived back in Virginia Jasmine went over to Thomas's aunt's house. His cousin asked Jasmine to babysit for a little while. Jasmine took Vincent and walked over to the apartment, so she could get ready for work at the same time.

Thomas came in the house a short time later and started calling Jasmine names. Jasmine grabbed Vincent and went to leave. Thomas blocked the door. Thomas started screaming at Jasmine and accusing her of sleeping with James while he was gone. Jasmine stood there in shock.

James was Jasmine's best friend's boyfriend. That was a line Jasmine never would cross. As Jasmine tried to walk away holding Vincent, Thomas slapped her in the face. Thomas took off running and Jasmine called James and her best friend to tell them about Thomas's ridiculous accusations.

James was furious he immediately walked over to Thomas's aunt's house and met Jasmine there knowing Thomas would be over there as well. James told Thomas that he would never sleep with Jasmine. Thomas told James he believed him. However, for weeks on end Thomas accused Jasmine of sleeping with James. He called Jasmine a whore and a slut bucket. He told her she was just a stupid whore and deserved to be treated the way he treated her. Jasmine began to believe him.

A week later the eviction on the apartment was finalized. Thomas moved his and Jasmine's stuff into his aunt's house and Jasmine began spending the night there. Jasmine and Thomas still had to attend their court date as well which came shortly after the eviction. Jasmine had been in touch with the lady from the stet dot program. She didn't know what would happen to Thomas in court. Thomas got probation before judgment and community service.

Jasmine was relieved neither of them had to do time in jail they both just had to stay out of trouble. Jasmine wasn't planning on getting into any more trouble, so she wasn't worried about it. One afternoon Jasmine stopped over at her dad's house to spend time with her siblings. While she was there her little brother, Richard, came inside and said that someone told him that the boys who stole his bike were down at the local elementary school. He wanted to go get his bike back. Jasmine agreed to go with him. While on the way

Jasmine ran into a few of Thomas's friends and they agreed to go with her because there was a gang turf war going on in the area at the time.

About one block from the elementary school Jasmine's phone rang. Her stepmom needed her to get to the house immediately. Jasmine's dad was being taken to the hospital by ambulance. Jasmine told her stepmom she would get there as fast as she could. Jasmine's only request was to keep the downstairs bathroom open so Jasmine could use the cold water when she got there. Jasmine knew her lungs wouldn't be able to handle the run and she would probably need a breathing treatment as well. Jasmine and Richard ran home as fast as they could. Sure, enough once they got to the house Jasmine ran into the downstairs bathroom and closed the door turning on the cold water to cool her skin and help return her respirations to normal.

Once EMS left to take Jasmine's dad to the hospital her stepmom asked her if she could stay the night with the kids. One of the neighbors brought over popsicles for the kids and Jasmine's stepmom gave her money to order pizza for the kids. Jasmine's dad was in the hospital for about two weeks. Jasmine had to take care of her siblings Michelle was the youngest and she was only 3 at the time. Michelle was so worried about her dad. Jasmine tried to put her at ease and spent some of her savings taking Michelle shopping to take her mind off things. Jasmine oversaw making the kids dinner, making sure they had lunch money, getting them to and from school, as well as making sure their homework was done. Three of the kids were under the age of ten the other two were in high school.

Once Jasmine's dad came home from the hospital Jasmine no longer had a job. Jasmine ended up moving back in with her dad and looking for a job. A few days later while Jasmine was at Thomas's house, she got a call that she needed to get Rainbow at the local mall as soon as possible because they wanted her to start work immediately. Jasmine quickly threw on clothes and went to the store to start her first day of work.

Jasmine enjoyed her new job. Some nights when Jasmine worked late the managers would drive her home. Jasmine and Thomas once again began having issues. Jasmine and Thomas were constantly arguing he was always accusing her of cheating. Thomas was constantly grabbing Jasmine and hitting her. One day he hit Jasmine before her shift at work, so she broke up with him. Thomas showed up at Jasmine's dad's house and left flowers with her stepmom for Jasmine. Jasmine told her stepmom to throw them away. Jasmine was livid how dare he hit her, and things flowers would solve everything and make it better. Jasmine's manager thought something seemed off because Thomas would pop up at the store all the time to make sure Jasmine was there or to see what time she was getting off.

Daniella, Jasmine's manager, eventually asked Jasmine if everything was alright. Jasmine assured her things were fine. The truth was Jasmine was looking for a way out. Jasmine just wanted to disappear. Jasmine was finally beginning to get up the courage to leave.

One morning Thomas almost made Jasmine late for work. Jasmine went over to Thomas's house to pick up her cell phone before heading to work. Thomas had a bad habit of taking Jasmine's phone. When Jasmine got to Thomas's house to get her phone, he started accusing her of cheating. Since Jasmine didn't have time to argue she grabbed her phone and went to leave. Thomas grabbed her purse and dumped it all over the floor. Jasmine bent down and picked everything up. Once again, she had to snatch her phone back from Thomas because he had taken it again. Thomas continued to take Jasmine's phone and dump her purse out several times. Jasmine didn't realize that Vincent was there with Thomas and was watching them fight from the steps. Eventually Thomas grabbed Jasmine by the throat and began strangling her. Jasmine couldn't breathe she felt as though she would black out at any moment. Jasmine knew it was now or never and she swung hitting Thomas in his left eye. Thomas was stunned for just long enough to allow Jasmine to grab her phone and purse and run out of the house.

A few moments after Jasmine arrived at the bus stop Thomas called Jasmine to ask if she had called the police because they were knocking on his front door. Jasmine told Thomas she didn't call and that it was probably one of his neighbors since they had been screaming and yelling in the house. Once Jasmine got to work Brittany called her cellphone. Jasmine answered not sure why Brittany was calling. Brittany asked Jasmine if she was okay. Jasmine said yes. Brittany went on to tell Jasmine that Vincent saw Thomas choke her and he was upset. Jasmine thought to herself I wonder if it was Vincent who called the police. Later that day when Jasmine went to lunch, she called Thomas and broke up with him she was tired of the constant fights and abuse.

That evening after work Jasmine didn't go home. There was a man name Mike who constantly asked Jasmine out. Jasmine went and spent the night at Mike's house after work. While she was there Thomas began calling Jasmine's phone repeatedly. He then called Jasmine's dad's house trying to speak with Jasmine. After Thomas called his house Jasmine's dad became worried and called Jasmine to make sure she was okay. Jasmine was. Her dad told her I know you are not with Thomas, so don't lie. I don't care where you are if you are okay. Jasmine told her dad she was fine and with some friends. Jasmine's dad told her that he had told Thomas she was sleeping. Jasmine's dad was far from dumb and knew that they had been fighting.

At this point Jasmine was done with Thomas and didn't care if she ever saw him again. Jasmine began hanging out with her childhood friends again. While hanging out with Jamal, who attended elementary school with Jasmine, Thomas approached. He was furious he attacked Jasmine and stole her coat and her phone. Jamal told Thomas he didn't know what his problem was, but whatever it was it wasn't worth it. Thomas took off running throwing the hood of Jasmine's coat up into a tree on his run. Jasmine was embarrassed.

An hour later Jasmine was hungry and wanted to eat, so Jamal and Jasmine walked to the shopping center. On the way to the shopping center Thomas attacked Jasmine again and shoved her to the ground. Jamal helped Jasmine up and they went to the carryout right across the street. What Jamal didn't know was that the owner of the carryout used to babysit Jasmine when she was younger.

Diana's husband went after Thomas to try to get her coat and phone back. Diana called the police. The police couldn't do anything because Jasmine wasn't injured. Jasmine felt defeated. Diana took down Jamal's cellphone number and gave Jasmine a salad to eat. Jasmine walked back over to Jamal's friend's house with him where she sat and ate her salad.

A little while later Jasmine's dad called Jamal's phone looking for her. Her dad was furious. He wanted to know where Jasmine was. Jasmine's dad came to pick her up and took her back home. On the way to get Jasmine he ran into Thomas. He and Thomas got into an argument and Jasmine's dad launched him into a fence. He wanted him to see how it felt to get picked on by someone twice his size. After her dad picked her up, he told her he was going to help Jasmine get a protective order against Thomas. Her dad asked her how she would feel if it were her baby sister, Michelle, in her shoes to Jasmine it wasn't that simple.

The next morning, Jasmine's dad drove her to work and walked her in. He spoke to both her manager Daniella as well as security. Jasmine's dad picked her up early from work to take her to the courthouse to file for an order of protection against Thomas. When they got to court Jasmine was granted a temporary order of protection Jasmine had a feeling Thomas would wiggle his way back into her life. Jamal had started working with Jasmine and drove her home one day after work. When Jasmine got to the door Thomas jumped out of a bush and grabbed her. Its scared Jasmine to death. She didn't know what to do. Jamal had already said he wouldn't testify against Thomas. When Jasmine went back to court for the final protective order hearing it was not granted. Jasmine blamed Jamal for refusing to testify.

Within two weeks Thomas had worked his way back into Jasmine's life. Around this same time Jasmine's job hired a male employee, David, to break down shipments. He was very sweet and noticed almost immediately that something was wrong in Jasmine and Thomas's relationship. One day Jasmine showed up to work and David noticed she had a black eye. David confronted Jasmine she told him she had no clue what he was talking about. Jasmine didn't even realize she had a black eye never mind how she got it.

Jasmine began trying to figure out how to escape. She began sleeping with one of the bus drivers, Tim, when her Thomas were "off". Tim was the opposite of Thomas he was tall, and sweet. He would always offer to hang out with Jasmine after work and give her free transfers so she wouldn't have to pay to take the bus to and from work every day. It didn't help matters that another bus driver, Kenny, tried to cause Thomas and Jasmine to fight.

Jasmine and Tim were always careful what they said to one another in front of the other bus drivers. However, Kenny always liked to cause problems. He would allow Thomas to hid eon the back of the bus and Thomas was very jealous. One day he saw Tim share his leftover lunch with Jasmine. Thomas lost it even though him and Jasmine weren't together at the time. Jasmine always made sure someone knew where she was after work. Typically, she would tell David if she was going out with Tim and then if David saw Thomas in the mall, he would call Jasmine to let her know. Thomas always thought that Jasmine was sleeping with David. David didn't care because he just wanted Jasmine safe.

Then a couple weeks later Jasmine was in an accident on the bus. She injured her lower back. She was in so much pain and had to rely on Thomas to take care of her because she couldn't work for two weeks and when she did go back, she was on light duty for another two weeks. When Jasmine started back to work things were fine at first, she started back lifting though only a few days in to her shifts because while Jasmine was out David got fired. Two weeks after starting back Jasmine started having lower back pain again. She figured it was from the accident and her manager if she could go home. The manager, Tina, told her that the district manager would be coming in to close the store so she would have to check with her when she came in around 6PM. Tina asked Jasmine if she had taken lunch yet. Jasmine told Tina she hadn't, but she really didn't feel well. Tina didn't care she told Jasmine to go take a lunch and come back and work the shoe department.

While on lunch Jasmine walked upstairs to Claire's and spoke to the manager Elsa to see if she had any openings. Elsa informed Jasmine that she would have a key carrier opening in the next few weeks and that she would be willing to hire Jasmine. While Jasmine was waiting to start at Claire's Thomas got arrested for a second time. This time it was worse. He was supposed to pick Jasmine up from work and never showed. Jasmine called her cell phone tons of times because Thomas had it and she still got no answer. Jasmine waited for 30 minutes before taking a cab to Thomas's house. Luckily, she had enough cash on her to cover the cost of the cab.

When Jasmine got to Thomas's house, she went in his room gathering her schoolbooks before heading to her dad's to go study and get some rest. While their Jasmine's dad called and asked Thomas's aunt if Jasmine or Thomas was at the house. She put Jasmine on the phone. Jasmine found out from her dad that Thomas had been arrested. Her dad found out because Jessica's cousin called her, and the police answered her phone and told her cousin his drug dealer was in police custody. Jasmine's cousin was concerned that Jasmine was in trouble. Jasmine told Thomas's aunt what her dad said, and she ended up calling him back and speaking to him about the situation. Jasmine was so mad Thomas was supposed to start community service the following day for his previous charge and he was on probation already.

Thomas was arrested on charges of possession with intent to distribute, possession of marijuana, and possession of paraphernalia. Thomas was with his friends outside drinking beer when the incident took place. Thomas then tried to run from the officers while tossing marijuana as he ran. However, when Thomas rounded a corner, he ran into two air conditioning units which then allowed the officer to place him under arrest.

Jasmine and Thomas's aunt were waiting for him to be given a bond once they found out what his bond amount was Jasmine gave Thomas's aunt $200 from his stash towards his bond, she tried to give his aunt more money, but she wouldn't take it. Thomas's uncle and Jasmine picked him up after he was released on bond and Jasmine was furious, she had to go to school, and she hadn't slept all night. Thomas's aunt was going to let him shower and then drive him to community service. Jasmine told her not to reward his bad behavior. Jasmine made him get dressed and take the bus to community service since she went past there on the bus anyway. Jasmine was so annoyed with Thomas that she had a zero-tolerance level with him that morning.

When Jasmine and Thomas got on the bus Thomas started talking to his friends. Tim was driving the bus and noticed Jasmine looked pissed. Jasmine looked at Thomas and told him, "Sit the hell down and shut up. I don't want to hear your voice right now." Tim gave Jasmine a look like wow is everything ok. Once Thomas was off the bus Jasmine explained to Tim what happened the night before he shook his head.

One-week later Jasmine started at Claire's. She was thrilled she enjoyed her new coworkers and the less stressful working environment. Jasmine also, enjoyed making more money and being full time.

CHAPTER SIX

BABY ON THE WAY

Two weeks after starting Claire's Jasmine didn't get her period. She took a pregnancy test at work one night, it was positive. That night after work Jasmine went to Thomas's house to tell him she was pregnant. She was nervous.

When Jasmine told Thomas, she was pregnant he demanded that she get an abortion. Jasmine refused. A couple of days later while Thomas was at community service Jasmine was lying in bed at Thomas's house she wasn't feeling well. Her head was pounding and the smell of the food his aunts were cooking was making her nauseous. Thomas's aunt, Sherry, walked past Thomas's room and asked Jasmine if she was pregnant. Jasmine didn't answer. Instead she waited for his aunt to come out of the bathroom and told her she needed to talk to her. Jasmine told her she was pregnant. His aunt asked why she hadn't said anything sooner. Jasmine explained that Thomas didn't want her to tell anyone he didn't want anyone to know.

That evening when Thomas got home from community service his aunt was on the phone telling his family in New York that Jasmine was pregnant. They were excited. Sherry heard Thomas come up the steps and she confronted him. He was livid. Thomas told Sherry that Jasmine was lying, and they weren't having a baby. Sherry knew not to listen to him, so she just ignored him.

At this point Jasmine realized she needed a second job and even though once Thomas was finished community service, he would have a full-time position at the Boys and Girls Club where he did his community service. She knew that Thomas and she needed to get an apartment. Jasmine got a second job at Payless shoes located in the same mall with Claire's. Working two jobs meant Jasmine had less time for Thomas. He was upset. In October 2008 Jasmine and Thomas moved into their own apartment. Jasmine was so excited her hard work had paid off.

The month after they moved in Jasmine got a promotion at work. Not only would she be making more money she was now full time. In order to do the paperwork for her raise and maternity leave Jasmine went in on her day off before her shift at Payless. Elsa and Jasmine quickly did the paperwork so that Jasmine could get over to Payless.

Jasmine walked down to the post office to mail her paperwork to corporate. As she rounded the hall to the post office, she heard Thomas's voice as his hand came across her face. Jasmine's first response was to bring her head down while covering her stomach to protect the baby. Thomas immediately took off. Jasmine walked back up to Claire's with a handprint across her face. It was taking everything inn her not to cry. Elsa saw Jasmine's face and asked the customer she was with to give her a moment.

Elsa gave Jasmine a hug and asked if she was hurt anywhere else. She looked up to see Thomas outside of the store. She told him he needed to leave the police were on the way. After Elsa finished with the customer, she called Thomas's aunt, Sherry. Sherry was furious and understood Elsa's concerns. She assured Elsa that she would handle it. Elsa had a gut feeling for some time that Thomas had been hurting Jasmine. After she knew Thomas was out of the mall Jasmine walked downstairs to Payless to work her four-hour shift.

After her shift Jasmine walked home almost hoping Thomas wouldn't come home that night. Shortly after Thomas got home and was accompanied by his mom and Sherry. Sherry wanted to speak with both Jasmine and Thomas because she wanted Thomas to know that his actions were inappropriate. Thomas tried to tell his aunt that Jasmine had been working off the clock. Jasmine replied, "Did you ask me why I was there? No, you just jumped to conclusions. I only went in to sign forms for my raise and to ensure that my maternity leave would kick in. Since the baby has already dropped Elsa wanted to get them done sooner rather than later in case she comes early." Thomas ignored her.

Thomas just wanted to argue. Sherry wasn't having it she interrupted him and told him that if he put his hands-on Jasmine again, she was going to beat him. Thomas's mom is deaf, however she understood what was going and smacked him before she left. Thomas just stood there dumbfounded like it was the first time in his life his mom had hit him.

Jasmine felt like Thomas's family had her back and would make sure that he didn't hurt her. Things stayed quiet between Jasmine and Thomas after that. In January, Jasmine cut down to working one job, Claire's, because it was full time. Elsa's son, Patrick, started walking Jasmine home from work which really made Thomas mad. Patrick told Thomas, "It's simple either you come pick Jasmine up, or if I can't walk her home, I will give her my knife the choice is yours."

About one week later when Jasmine left work she got home to find Thomas's friend and girlfriend as well as their two children asleep under the steps in front of the apartment. Jasmine quickly went around back. She went inside the apartment and began cooking dinner for Thomas and herself. She then called Thomas's job to tell him to come in the back as well. Thomas had already left so Jasmine sat in the bathroom with the window open waiting for Thomas. Thomas got home and came in the back door. Jasmine finished cooking and then Thomas and she went and sat in their bedroom to eat. Jasmine wouldn't have minded letting his friends in; however, she was tired and they didn't have enough food to feed his friends and their children.

Thomas's family threw Jasmine a baby shower at his job. The only people that were invited from Jasmine's family were her mom, stepmom, and her two half siblings. Jasmine felt awkward at the shower while she knew some of the people there, she didn't know everyone, and it wasn't how she had imagined her baby shower. Thomas spent most of the time with his friends.

During the shower Thomas's sister's son began chasing Jasmine's sibling around with a board that had nails sticking out of it because no one was watching him. Thomas's sister was mad that Jasmine's stepmom said something about her son being out of control and began screaming at her and threatening her in the middle of the shower. Jasmine lost it she began crying and walked away at the point Jasmine's mom and stepmom told Jasmine they were going to head, and they apologized. Jasmine felt horrible they were the only ones there from Jasmine's side of the family and they were leaving. Jasmine was ready to go home.

When Jasmine left the room, Thomas began screaming at his sister. His sister continued to act like she wasn't in the wrong, so Thomas threw a cup of cold water on her and told her to calm down. Jasmine just shook her head she was completely over the entire day. Thomas's sister told someone to apologize for her and everyone told her she needed to apologize for herself. After everyone finished cleaning up a few people went back to Thomas's and Jasmine's apartment for cake.

The next day Jasmine went in to work and Elsa got a phone call that Patrick had been stabbed multiple times. Jasmine told Elsa to go and she would cover the store. Jasmine was nine months pregnant. Patrick got stabbed twice during a two-week period, once by gang members and the second time by his girlfriend's uncle. Patrick had become like a brother to Jasmine so she didn't mind holding down the fort at the store so his mom could be there with him at the hospital.

A few weeks later was Valentine's Day. Jasmine had to work a double because the manager was out sick, and the key carrier had already made plans and was out of town. Jasmine didn't care she was hoping Elsa would get better quickly and get back to work before Jasmine had the baby.

Four days later Jasmine went to see her doctor. They were going to induce her on the 22nd of February if she hadn't gone into labor yet.

Jasmine left the doctor's and went to let Elsa know what they had said. She had to use the restroom and noticed a little bit of blood and mucus when she wiped. Elsa told her that baby is coming I'll see you back at work in six weeks. Jasmine went ahead and called her doctor who had her come back to the office right as it was time for them to close. Her doctor checked her and told her to go home eat dinner walk around a little bit and then head to the hospital around 8:30 PM. Jasmine did.

Jasmine's doctor was a little concerned that Jasmine couldn't feel her contractions and told Jasmine that she had been having contractions that morning as well. The hospital didn't want to keep Jasmine, however, due to her medical condition her doctor convinced them to keep her. Jasmine's entire family was at the hospital waiting to see what was going to happen once they told them Jasmine was being admitted, but that baby wasn't coming that night they all went home.

Jasmine managed to hold off on getting an epidural until 6AM then she was in so much pain she couldn't take it. When they did the epidural Jasmine's, water broke half way. Around 8 AM Jasmine's mom, dad, and stepmom reappeared at the hospital to wait for the baby's arrival. Jasmine's doctor showed around 9 and checked Jasmine, she broke Jasmine's water the rest of the way and told everyone not to expect a baby until around 6 PM. However, Nikki made her appearance at 1:29 PM. She was beautiful. Jasmine didn't waste any time and started nursing Nikki right away.

Nikki was a good baby she slept through the night and was never fussy. Jasmine started back to school exactly one week after giving birth. Thomas kept Nikki while Jasmine was in class. As much as Jasmine enjoyed being off work with Nikki, she missed her coworkers, so she spent a lot of time taking Nikki to visit them.

CHAPTER SEVEN

TIME TO GO BACK TO WORK

The first six weeks of Nikki's life Jasmine and Thomas didn't argue at all Jasmine could come and go from the house as she pleased while Thomas was at work. On Monday and Wednesday nights Jasmine had class at the local college she started back only a few days after having Nikki. Jasmine had dinner on the table when Thomas got home every night. However, when she started back to work things changed. Jasmine's stepmom would babysit while Jasmine worked during the day. Jasmine worked long hours especially once she went back because they were down one employee then Elsa got very sick. When Elsa got sick Jasmine had to work twelve hour shifts every day to cover the store. The day of her little brother's graduation Jasmine got called in because she had someone covering from another store and Jasmine's key carrier who was supposed to fill in that afternoon called out.

Jasmine's work schedule started arguments between Thomas and her. First Thomas would complain that she was always at work. One morning when Nikki was only two months old Jasmine woke up and Nikki was running a fever. Thomas had been out partying the night before and had a hangover. He expected Jasmine to get up and call him out of work because he had a hangover. Jasmine was dealing with Nikki and trying to get her in to see her doctor. Jasmine was furious. Thomas called his aunt to complain that Jasmine wouldn't call him out of work. His aunt said Thomas should go to the appointment with you. Jasmine told his aunt Thomas said he isn't going to the doctor with her and Nikki; he is staying home to sleep. Thomas cared more about his hangover than he did about his two-month old running a fever.

Jasmine took the baby to the doctor and got some medicine for her. Jasmine got back home and took care of the baby for her that was the last straw she was done. She wanted to make things work until the lease ended in September. Jasmine had to make it work for five more months. The following month Thomas's aunt watched Nikki one day while Jasmine and Thomas were both at work. Thomas had gotten home and went out after Jasmine had told his aunt to head over with the baby. This created big problems for Jasmine. By the time Jasmine got to the house his cousin Stephanie was livid. Stephanie began yelling and screaming at Jasmine because no one had been home to get the baby. Jasmine was annoyed she was done Thomas couldn't sit in the house and get his daughter, instead he went to the liquor store to get a bottle of Hennessy. While his cousin Brittany was holding Nikki during the heated argument Jasmine grabbed everything she could for Nikki. She then took Nikki from Brittany and she left crying. Jasmine walked back up to her job looked at Elsa and asked to stay with her that night. Elsa said yes. Jasmine had to stop at the store to grab diapers for Nikki, but other than that she had bottles, formula, and everything else she needed for Nikki. Jasmine had become beyond fed up. The next day when Jasmine went home Thomas. had locked her out of the apartment. Jasmine had to find maintenance to let her back inside.

One night while Jasmine was closing at work, she couldn't reach Thomas. She called his aunt's house. His aunt sent her husband and Thomas's cousin, May, to pick Jasmine up from work. His aunt had been watching Nikki. Before May and Thomas's uncle arrived, Thomas appeared out of nowhere and started beating on the windows and gate of Jasmine's store. Jasmine was terrified she quickly called Thomas's aunt to tell her what was unfolding. The Macy's security guard, Chris, began yelling at Thomas because he was afraid for Jasmine's safety. Thomas's aunt had her husband and May go into the mall to get Jasmine. The Macy's security guard then escorted them out since he was trying to lock up the store.

As they were getting into the car Thomas jumped into the backseat with Jasmine and started punching her. May jumped out and switched places with Jasmine. When everyone was back in the car Thomas began trying to punch Jasmine still his uncle stopped the car. Thomas's aunt had called May to make sure Jasmine was in the car. May told her aunt how Thomas was behaving. Thomas refused to speak with his aunt, so May put the phone on speaker. His aunt told him, "If you cause my husband to have an accident, I will beat your ass." Once back at his aunt's house she told Thomas he had to stop his ridiculous behavior, or he would end up in jail. He agreed, however, his behavior never changed.

In August, Thomas decided that he was in another one of his moods and Jasmine had to be cheating on him so as she was walking home from work one day, he began throwing rocks at her. Passerby's called the police so Jasmine walked back to her job to catch the bus to Thomas's aunt's house. The police stopped her along the way. The officers asked her if everything was alright and Jasmine told them she was fine. Deep inside though Jasmine wasn't fine she knew she needed a way out and fast. What was she going to do? She couldn't afford a place right now. Jasmine got to Thomas's aunt's house and his aunt pretended that Jasmine never showed to get Nikki. When Thomas showed up his aunt yelled at him once again for his actions. She told him he was going to end up in jail. Thomas was mad at Jasmine for not telling him she was at his aunt's. Jasmine and Nikki stayed with his aunt that night because his aunt feared for their safety.

The next night when Jasmine got home from work, she brought Chinese food with her. Thomas was in a bad mood. He threw Jasmine's food on the floor and broke picture frames holding pictures of Nikki. Afraid for both her and Nikki's safety Jasmine called Thomas's aunt. She was hoping his aunt would be able to get Thomas to go stay with her for the night and cool down. Instead his aunt ended up taking Nikki home with her and Jasmine started cleaning up. Thomas came in and out of the house a few times fighting with Jasmine. Finally, Jasmine got him out of the house, and she pushed both couches against the front door. Then she pushed the kitchen table and chairs against the back door. Jasmine then went in their bedroom locked the door and went to sleep.

The next day Jasmine went and reapplied for her position at Payless. She knew if she was going to get her own place, she would need to have two jobs. Jasmine was working two jobs and going to school and caring for a small infant. Jasmine was a mess; mentally, physically, and emotionally and no one knew. Jasmine hid her feelings very well. A couple days later Jasmine asked Patrick to accompany her to social services so she could apply for assistance with her security deposit and first month's rent on a new apartment. Her lease was going to be up at the end of September, and she wanted her own place. Patrick went with Jasmine and Nikki. Afterwards Jasmine went with Patrick to Claire's to take Nikki to see Elsa. After their visit with Elsa, Patrick carried Nikki home because Jasmine had her hands full. Thomas's friends saw Patrick carrying Nikki and called him. Thomas was furious. Thomas began paying people to follow Jasmine. Patrick caught one of the young boys Thomas had paid. Patrick told the boy to stay away from Jasmine. Patrick also, confronted Thomas and told him nothing better happen to Jasmine.

The next morning after Thomas was out of the shower Jasmine went to shower and get ready for work since Nikki was still asleep. While Jasmine was in the shower Thomas took dirty clothes, the kitchen chairs, and Nikki's play pen and piled them in front of the bathroom door. Thomas didn't stop there he poured an entire bottle of baby powder on everything. It was almost impossible for Jasmine to get out of the bathroom without becoming covered in powder. Jasmine got out of the bathroom and gathered her and Nikki's dirty laundry. She then asked her stepmom to wash it warning her to be careful as everything was covered in baby powder. Jasmine also, quickly vacuumed the floor before leaving for work.

That night after Jasmine got home from work, she sensed Thomas wanted to argue so she called her dad and asked him to pick her and Nikki up. Jasmine and Nikki went and stayed with her dad that night. The following night when Thomas got home from work Jasmine was already home trying to sleep, she was tired and had a migraine. Thomas plopped Nikki down on the bed causing the entire to bed to shake. When Jasmine told him to stop because she didn't feel well Thomas responded, "Bitch suck my dick!" Jasmine told him no and rolled over to go back to sleep after moving Nikki so she wouldn't fall. Thomas then said, "After I get out of the shower my boys are coming over and we are going to run a train on you." Jasmine had enough. She got up, waited for Thomas to get out of the shower and left for the store. While she was at the store, she called her dad once again and told him to come get her and Nikki.

That night Jasmine's dad said, "I am not coming out every night to get you and Nikki. Why don't you and Nikki move back in with me?" Jasmine agreed she knew that to protect both herself and Nikki she needed to move back home.

CHAPTER EIGHT

MOVING BACK HOME

The next two days while Thomas was working Jasmine and her stepmom moved Jasmine and Nikki back home with Jasmine's dad. Once Thomas realized that Jasmine was gone, and they were over for good he began harassing Jasmine at work. He would call her while she was at Claire's at threaten to trash the store and flip the display cases over. Elsa notified security. Thomas would call Jasmine's cell phone and leave Jay-Z, Mary J. Blige, and Keisha Cole lyrics on her voice mail. He would even call her to tell her she is a whore, slut, or a bitch. When that no longer hurt Jasmine, Thomas began calling and saying Jasmine raped him.

Towards the end of September, Jasmine felt sympathy for Thomas she went over his house to stay the night to attempt to work things out. That was a huge mistake. The first thing Thomas said Jasmine was, "Don't kiss Nikki we don't know where your mouth has been." Jasmine ignored him and went inside the apartment to shower. While she was in the shower Thomas came in the bathroom and stood there talking to her. He was trying to argue. When his attempts at arguing failed he began lighting matches and throwing them at Jasmine while she was in the shower. Jasmine felt very vulnerable as she had nothing to protect her except the water from the shower which could turn cold at any time. Jasmine wanted to cry. She asked herself why I even bothered trying to work things out. She knew deep inside she should have left well enough alone. Luckily, for Jasmine Thomas ran out of matches before the water got cold.

In October, Jasmine was finally able to get her own place. She moved in which opened her up for more abuse. Thomas came to drop Nikki off one night. Jasmine only opened the door enough to grab Nikki from him she didn't want him pushing his way inside. Thomas pushed the door open further and hit Jasmine with the door. Two days later when he came to drop Nikki off Thomas spit in Jasmine's face as she took the baby from him. Jasmine was beyond annoyed she was really beginning to hate him.

On October 17, 2009 Thomas did the unbelievable. Thomas called Jasmine before she headed into work and said, "Bring me my fucking daughter." He then called back ten minutes later and told Jasmine, "If you bring Nikki here, I have a cup of shit and a cup of piss waiting on you." To avoid conflict all together Jasmine left Nikki in the house with a friend. When Jasmine reached the top of her street Thomas jumped out from behind a tree and punched Jasmine in the back of the head and stole her phone. Jasmine then walked back home to use her friend's phone to call the police. The police came out and took a police report as you can see below. No charges were ever filed against Thomas for this incident.

On November 18, 2009 Thomas brought Nikki back home once he left, he called Jasmine's cellphone and threatened to stab her and her boyfriend. Jasmine was scared she didn't know what to do. She went and filed for a temporary protective order against Thomas. Once Jasmine filed for an order of protection Thomas went and filed for one against her alleging that she elbowed him while they were arguing face to face. In this same report he also stated that Jasmine's father had threatened to kill him. On November 24, 2009 a final protective order was issued. Jasmine thought she would begin feeling safe once again.

CHAPTER NINE

JEALOUSY SETS IN

In January 2010, Thomas saw Jasmine getting off the bus with Nikki and another man. He was livid. He followed Jasmine and the man to Jasmine's apartment. Once they were inside Thomas began beating on Jasmine's windows. He didn't stop there he started screaming at the top of his lungs outside of her apartment. Jasmine knew if she called the police, they wouldn't do anything, and it would take them forever to respond. Jasmine called Patrick. By the time Patrick got there Thomas was gone. Patrick talked to Jasmine for a few minutes and then went back home. After that Jasmine was constantly on the look-out for Thomas. If Jasmine heard a noise outside, she was in the window expecting to find Thomas standing there watching her apartment. Jasmine felt helpless.

One Tuesday night when Jasmine went to leave for school, she saw Thomas outside in the alley between her apartment and the college. Jasmine ended up missing school that night in fear of getting injured trying to make it to school. Thomas made Jasmine's life impossible. He wanted to control her every move. In April 2010 Jasmine moved back in with her dad. She was tired of dealing with Thomas and his nonsense, not to mention Claire's had closed so she could no longer afford to pay her rent.

One day in May, Jasmine dropped Nikki off to Thomas and went to Kroger before getting on the bus to go to work. On the way to Kroger Jasmine noticed Thomas was chasing after her. Jasmine quickly went into Kroger hoping it would prevent Thomas from hurting her. Thomas ran up behind Jasmine punched her in the back of the head and said, "It's a stick up give me all of your money." Jasmine burst into tears she was humiliated the employees just stood there staring, no one moved.

Jasmine called a friend and walked out to the bus stop because she still had to go to work. While at the bus stop Thomas approached Jasmine a second time. This time he got in her face and kicked the bag with her groceries in it knocking her soda out of the bag. Jasmine asked Thomas several times to stop and to leave her alone he refused. He then kicked the soda across the street where he began to shake the soda up. Thomas then proceeded to walk to the middle of the street begin unscrewing the soda and threw it at Jasmine. Jasmine was already flustered, and Thomas had just made it worse. Jasmine got off the phone with her friend and got on the bus.

The following week while Thomas had Nikki for the weekend Jasmine walked to Kroger with her little sister, Sara to get diapers, wipes, and food for Nikki. When they were on the way to the store Sara informed her that Nikki and Thomas were behind them. Jasmine told her not to worry about it and to just keep walking they were going to hurry up. Once inside the store as usual Thomas had to start something. Thomas walked up to Jasmine and called her a slut in front of both Sara and Nikki. Sara told Thomas he was mean and that he should be beat.

A few days later Jasmine was on the bus going home from work. Thomas boarded the bus by the Motel 6, which is known for prostitution and drugs. Once on the bus Thomas called Jasmine a slut bucket as he got on. Thomas could never just not say anything when he saw Jasmine. Even with the protective order in place he just didn't know how to keep his mouth shut.

Then on August 22, 2010 Thomas's aunt called Jasmine she said that Thomas's sister, Amber, wanted to Nikki to go to Sesame Place with them from Thursday to Sunday. Jasmine agreed. Nikki was supposed to be gone from August 26 to August 29. However, while Nikki was still with them Amber called and said that they were still in Sesame Place. Jasmine told her that was fine Nikki just needed to be home before her playgroup on Thursday morning. Per the protective order Nikki was to be dropped off Wednesday night at 8pm. While Jasmine was at work on Wednesday Thomas called her numerous asking her to pick up Nikki. When he called Jasmine told him Elsa would be more than happy to watch Nikki, he just had to drop her off. When Jasmine got home from work, she had dinner and waited outside until 8:15 pm for Nikki. When Nikki didn't show she called Thomas's aunt.

His aunt said, "I don't know when Nikki will be home. Didn't you speak to Amber?" Ten minutes later Amber called demanding to know why Jasmine was stressing her aunt out. Jasmine told her she just wanted to know when Nikki would be home as Thomas had been calling Jasmine all day telling her to come get Nikki. up all day that day. Amber told Jasmine that Thomas would bring Nikki home whenever he felt like it. Jasmine then told Amber that if Nikki was not home by the following morning, she would be pressing charges as per the protective order Nikki should have been home.

Jasmine got Nikki back the following morning. Nikki was very aggressive when she returned. Nikki came home and started pushing Sara to the ground something she had never done before. Jasmine had to teach Nikki that she couldn't push Sara. So, every time Nikki pushed Sara, Nikki was put in timeout.

On October 9, 2010 Nikki went to Thomas's as per the protective order and while Jasmine was at work on October 10 Thomas's aunt left her a voice mail. The voice mail said that Nikki would be dropped back off at home on the 11th because his aunt was out of town. Jasmine then called his aunt back to request that they drop Nikki off to her parents. When Jasmine returned his aunt's call, she was informed that they took Nikki out of state without permission and now had to extend their visitation.

The following week Thomas had Nikki for an overnight during the week. Jasmine stayed out with some friends so she wouldn't have to pay to take the bus to work. When Thomas called her Deon answered her phone. Jasmine was in the bathroom. Thomas was furious because she was with Deon, Patrick, and their friends. Thomas started demanding Jasmine come to pick up Nikki immediately.

Deon knew Jasmine didn't have money for the bus, so he told Thomas, "If we come to get Nikki you are getting your ass beat when we get there." That ended that. The next day however, while Jasmine was at work Thomas decided to pay Deon a visit. Thomas took Nikki with him. Thomas pulled a gun on Deon threatening to shoot him. Deon let it be because Nikki was there. Deon knew if anything happened to Nikki Jasmine and Patrick would be on a war path.

Then on October 26, 2010 Thomas was waiting at the bus stop when Jasmine approached. Jasmine knew to keep her distance from Thomas and walked past him directly up to the bus stop sign. She was on the phone with her friend Eric, who lived in New York. Thomas was also, on his phone when he saw Jasmine, he told whomever he was speaking with, "My stupid whore of a baby mother is at the bus stop…" Jasmine ignored him continuing to talk to Eric.

Thomas then picked up a pine cone and threw it at Jasmine. Jasmine kindly asked Thomas not to throw things at her. He laughed and started walking towards Jasmine. Jasmine backed away but not fast enough he reached in her pocket grabbed her money and threw it all over the ground. Jasmine picked it up and went and stood closer to the road this time. Before Jasmine could move Thomas ran up behind her trying to shove her in the street to get her phone. Jasmine got away with only a scratch on her hand. Jasmine went and hid behind an electrical box as he ran down the street. Jasmine called 911.

While Jasmine was on the phone with the dispatcher Thomas began throwing rocks at Jasmine. Then he began yelling across the street that he was going to shoot Jasmine.

Once the police arrived on scene Thomas called Jasmine's phone. The officers asked him to come back to the scene he told the officers no and began taunting them. The officers asked Jasmine why there were pinecones and rocks scattered everywhere. Jasmine explained that Thomas had been throwing them at her.

Jasmine's stepmom pulled up and ended up driving Jasmine to work. Once at work Stephanie called Jasmine to make sure she was okay. Her neighbors had called her because the police had showed looking for Thomas and were all over their block. Jasmine told Stephanie what happened, and that she was okay.

CHAPTER TEN

CUSTODY BATTLE

In December 2010, Jasmine decided to move out of Alexandria to further distance herself from Thomas. She moved back in with her mother to watch her nephew while her older stepsister was at work. Jasmine was excited to be able to move away from Thomas. She knew that Thomas would never be able to cause her any harm once she moved to Alexandria. Jasmine was very excited to start this new chapter in her life.

In December as Jasmine was moving, the Richmond Police Department issued a warrant for Thomas's arrest. When the warrant detectives went to serve the warrant, Stephanie told the detectives that Thomas and Jasmine were back together. The warrant detectives then reached out to Jasmine's stepmother who informed the detectives that Jasmine had moved to Alexandria to get away from Thomas. The detective then contacted Jasmine to ensure that she knew Thomas had an active warrant for his arrest. Once

Jasmine was notified, she ceased all visitations between Nikki and Thomas in fear for Nikki's safety.

Thomas was arrested on February 17, 2011 for the warrant and possession of marijuana. While he was in jail for the violation of the protective order Thomas was served papers stating that Jasmine had filed for custody. Jasmine added fuel to the fire. Her hope was though that since Thomas was running from the warrant that the police wouldn't be able to find him to serve the papers. The conditions of Thomas's bond were that he could have no contact with Jasmine. That still didn't stop him.

On June 18, 2011 Thomas approached Jasmine at the bus stop and stood inches from her face to ask her how she was doing. Jasmine responded, "Leave me alone you are violating your bond." Deep inside Thomas knew he was getting under Jasmine's skin and he enjoyed every moment of it. On June 20, 2011 Thomas walked inside Jasmine's job at Payless and stood in line behind her customers just smiling at her. Jasmine excused herself from assisting her customer walked from behind the register and demanded that he leave the store immediately. Once again, she told him was in violation of his bond.

Each time Jasmine contacted the Alexandria Prosecutor's Office to make them aware of the situation. She knew this was a dangerous game and she did not want to be dealt the short end of the stick. The prosecutor's office agreed, and they issued a warrant due to bond revocation. When Jasmine went to court on July 20th for the assault charges, he plead incompetent to stand trial.

During the trial for the violation of the order of protection Jasmine and Thomas were also, going to court for custody. Thomas tried to use everything he could think of against Jasmine. Once the initial hearing occurred Jasmine and Thomas both had to speak to the court evaluator. Since Jasmine lived in Alexandria the court evaluator came out to her house.

When the evaluator arrived, Jasmine showed her around the house and introduced her to everyone who lived there at the time. She wanted to see what Jasmine and Nikki's morning routine was at the time. After showing the evaluator around Jasmine set up the laptop for Nikki and together, they worked through some different educational programs for children with Autism since Nikki had been diagnosed with developmental delays. The evaluator was impressed.

The week of Thomas's visit Jasmine had a lot going on. Jasmine's dad was out of town, she had to work, and she had to prepare for the custody case. She rearranged her work schedule around when her dad needed her to keep her siblings and around court. Thomas's visit with the evaluator was this week and Nikki needed to be present. Jasmine got up that morning got the children off to school, fed Nikki and left from Richmond to Alexandria to take Nikki to the evaluation.

When Jasmine got to the courthouse the evaluator was calling her, she was livid. Jasmine told the evaluator she was downstairs and would be up in a moment. When Jasmine got upstairs the evaluator told her Thomas's aunt thought the meeting was the following day. His attorney called her to see what could be done. Jasmine explained to the evaluator that she was taking care of five other children and Nikki. She had schedules to keep, but she would have Nikki's uncle bring her to the meeting the following day.

The next day at the evaluation Nikki had to be forced to go back with Thomas. Once in the room Thomas had to be prompted to take out toys and interact with Nikki. The evaluator also, noted that he allowed her to color with markers all over herself and clothes. She also, wrote that Thomas had to bring photos of his house and he could not tell her what the photos were of. She also, went on to state that Nikki didn't have her own bed to sleep in and that would be an issue as she got older. The evaluator was not impressed by Thomas's performance at all.

A few weeks later Thomas and Jasmine went to court to hear the evaluators findings. Well things were in Jasmine's favor. The evaluator agreed that Thomas should be granted two short visitations during the week and visitation every other weekend. She also, indicated that all visitation should take place at his aunt's house. Jasmine was intrigued when the evaluator also, stated at the meeting that Thomas refused to take a drug test. Jasmine knew he wouldn't take one. Jasmine left this meeting looking responsible. Jasmine knew she was doing the best she could as a single mother. The truth was even though Jasmine had been through a lot she was a strong woman.

Jasmine and Thomas settled the custody agreement the morning it was to go before a judge. The judge signed off on the case. A copy of the agreement is included below. Jasmine was happy she got everything she had wanted. Deep down Jasmine had hoped Thomas would just sign his writes over however, everyone knew that wasn't going to happen.

CHAPTER ELEVEN

THE LIES JASMINE TOLD HERSELF

When Jasmine finally got the courage to leave, she was afraid and nervous. She knew in her heart that she was putting her life in more danger by leaving however, Jasmine needed to leave before she ended up dead. Jasmine knew this was no longer about her it was about Nikki.

Jasmine's life didn't get easier because she left her abuser. She had to learn to co-parent with him as well. However, Jasmine learned a lot from this experience. Jasmine decided she would never just settle again. Jasmine learned self-worth. While Jasmine did take out a protective order against Thomas, she knew that alone wouldn't save her.

As Jasmine reflected over her relationship with Thomas, she realized she lost herself and lied to herself often along the way. Jasmine didn't think there was an issue with Thomas's jealousy or with the way he spoke to her. When the abuse was solely verbal Jasmine didn't think it was abuse because he hadn't hit her. Jasmine now realizes that abuse is abuse. Jasmine always told herself, "Sticks and stones may break your bones, but words will never hurt me." Jasmine quickly taught herself to forget that saying after she left Thomas.

Jasmine realized through talking to friends she has gained over the years and from books like those by Rachel Hollis that she is worth more so much more than anything Thomas could have given her. Jasmine is by no means sorry for who she has become today. Jasmine thought while her and Thomas were together that if she would have followed his rules, she would have been fine. She blamed herself for their arrests. She even thought that she was stupid and deserved to be used as his personal punching bag. Jasmine convinced herself it was safer to stay then leave. Jasmine believed she was ugly and the way he spoke to her was a result of how ugly she was. Jasmine even told herself that name calling is not abuse.

Throughout her relationship with Thomas Jasmine made up excuses for his behavior and wouldn't see herself as a victim. Today though Jasmine realizes that if she wouldn't have left when she did, she could have been killed. Jasmine has found a calling for making sure that other women like herself never end up in a situation like this and if they do they know that there are other women who have been through it and are willing to listen to them and help them in any way they can. For Jasmine sharing her story with those around her is a way of helping not only herself, but those around her.

Jasmine has been raising Nikki to be a strong an independent young lady. Jasmine has taught Nikki self-respect and to not allow others to walk all over her. Jasmine herself has learned to stand up for herself she has self-confidence and self-respect. Years ago, when men would ask for naked pictures of her Jasmine would quickly send them so they would accept her and want to keep her around. Jasmine could care less what people think of her any more. She is happy in her skin and this experience has shaped who she is today. Jasmine graduated in 2014 from Kaplan University with an Associate's Degree in Health Information Technology. She also attended ISSA and received a personal training certification in 2019. She is going to be starting back to school in July of 2019 to obtain a fitness nutrition certification, so that she can continue helping women around the world build their self-confidence, self-respect, and self-esteem.

Jasmine is currently in a relationship and Nikki is still her only child. When it comes to finding love ladies Jasmine wants you to know to stop looking for it. You will find it when the time is right. Jasmine wasn't looking for a relationship when this one found her. What started out as rides home from work from a friend of a friend turned into so much more. Jasmine appreciates this relationship so much more than any other she had because it didn't start off based on sex. It was since they were attracted to one another on an intellectual level. Her current boyfriend has even accepted Nikki and they spend tons of time together. He babysits for Jasmine on occasion when she must work, and Nikki is out of school.

Ladies don't ever let a man control you it is the mistake Jasmine made. When you see a red flag, or you think something is not right trust your gut and run for the door. Don't think because he doesn't hit you it isn't abuse. Abuse can be verbal, physical, emotional, and even sexual. All of them are wrong and have no business in a relationship. Ladies I beg you to value yourself and if you need help please get it. Listed below is National Domestic Violence Hotline's phone number. I don't want to hear of any other women being killed by their partners. I don't want to hear of any other women being hospitalized or almost killed by their partners. It is time to take a stand a say enough is enough ladies. Please for the sake of you and your children please get out at the first sign of abuse.

National Domestic Violence Hotline: 844-443-5732 They are open 24 hours a day 7 days a week. If you need help, please call them and never be afraid to call 911 if you need help either ladies, they can help you get out as long as you are honest with them and yourself.

Printed in the United States
By Bookmasters